Acting Edition

Savage World

by Stephen Fife

FOR PRODUCTION INQUIRIES

UNITED STATES AND CANADA
info@concordtheatricals.com
1-866-979-0447

UNITED KINGDOM AND EUROPE
licensing@concordtheatricals.co.uk
020-7054-7298

Each title is subject to availability from Concord Theatricals Corp., depending upon country of performance. Please be aware that *SAVAGE WORLD* may not be licensed by Concord Theatricals Corp. in your territory. Professional and amateur producers should contact the nearest Concord Theatricals Corp. office or licensing partner to verify availability.

SAVAGE WORLD was first produced on October 17, 2008 at the Met Theatre in Hollywood, California. The performance was directed by L. Flint Esquerra, with Paul Koslo and Stephen Fife as producers. The costume designer was Dawn Worrall. The production stage manager and lights operator was Lloyd Reese. The cast was as follows:

CALVIN "SAVAGE" JAMES . . . . Vincent Ward

SOLOMON "SOL" EISNER . . . . .Erik Passoja

DETECTIVE FRANK SLEZAK . . . . John Del Regno

JACK EISNER . . . . .Tom Badal

ADELE SPARKS . . . . .Latarsha Rose

TYRONE BELL (AND OTHER ROLES) . . . . Roger Bridges

DANNY (SOL'S SON) / BUSTER (OTHERS). . . . . Nate Geez

MEL THOMAS / HARLEY MACK /
VERNON TATE (OTHERS) . . . . Ernest Harden, Jr.

JIMMY LUGO / MAXIE LAZLO /
MAN IN RAINCOAT / CREECH (OTHERS) . . . . Gary Colon

TED ROOKS / RAY BRANIFF /
BARRY SCHWARTZ (OTHERS) . . . . Darin Dahms

ELLA / CARLY / WAITRESS /
WOMAN MOTORIST / POLICEWOMAN (OTHERS) . . . Kathryn J. Taylor

MARSHA CONNER / TINA /
BELINDA / WENDY WHITE (OTHERS). . . . . Elain Rinehart

MAN IN RAINCOAT / MAXIE LAZLO. . . . . .Barry Shay

MARSHA CONNOR / TINA . . . . .Eileen Grubba

Script Development/Readings

Shenandoah Playwrights (VA), Kennedy Center (DC), Primary Stages, Westside Arts (NYC), alt. selection for the O'Neill/National Playwrights Conference. Big thanks to director Flint Esquerra.

CHARACTERS

CALVIN "SAVAGE" JAMES – Male, 35-45, African-American, a feared boxer.

YOUNG SOL EISNER – Male, 25-30, white, an investigative journalist.

SOLOMON "SOL" EISNER – In 2019-2020, male, 60-65, white. This actor also plays small roles in the other stage reality of the late 1970s: **COUNTY GUARD, PRISON GUARD, MAXIE LAZLO**.

DETECTIVE FRANK SLEZAK / TV FIGHT ANNOUNCER – Male, forties, white.

TYRONE BELL / DANNY (SOL'S SON) – Male, 40, African-American.

JIMMY LUGO / RAY BRANIFF / HOTEL BARTENDER / ROOKS / BARRY BARKER / CREECH / BERNARD / GUARD 2 – Male, 35-40, white or Latino.

ADELE SPARKS / ELLA / WOMAN MOTORIST – Female, 35, African-American.

BELINDA / TINA / POLLY / TV REPORTER / POLICEWOMAN / LA DJ / RADIO NEWS – Female, 33-38, white or Latina.

SETTING & TIME

The play takes place in dual times and places:

Trenton State Maximum Security Prison and other locations (mostly in New Jersey) from 1978-80 (except for one in 1967), and Park Slope, Brooklyn in "The Present" (early 2020, pre-pandemic)

AUTHOR'S NOTES

The play requires a bare-bones set that will suggest various locations with minimal settings and props. Must allow for fluid transitions.

For music: late Miles Davis ("Tutu" & "Decoy") and '70s tunes are suggested, but will require clearance from the rights holders.

Casting Notes

While this is a memory play, its genre is Realism, in two time periods. At its core, it deals with issues of Race, so I am against color-blind casting. There is some latitude, however, in casting the man and woman in their thirties who play several roles. Slezak could also be non-white, as he is merely the errand boy for higher-ups. For the two actors who play several roles: each character needs to be a distinct sketch. Keep them separate. Go with your first impulse.

For my dad, Marty Fife, who kept urging me to write a good story that everyone can relate to. I hope that this would have checked that box for him.

ACT I

Scene One

(Pre-set: A webcam, downstage center. Also, a small, blank screen or monitor, above and away from the stage action.)

(Also a door unit downstage right.)

(Houselights down. Sound of a loud knock on a wooden door.)

(December 2019. Brooklyn. Lights up on the door unit. Door open: **SOLOMON EISNER,** *sixties, on the inside, faces* **ELLA,** *thirty-six, Black, middle-class, on the outside.)*

ELLA. Danny's gone.

SOL. What do you mean, Danny's gone?

ELLA. I mean he quit his teaching job, and he left me and JJ.

SOL. Left you? As in moved out?

ELLA. Yeah! As in took all the damn stuff he cares about and shut the door behind him.

SOL. Why? What happened? You had a fight?

ELLA. That's not the point.

SOL. How come I'm only hearing about this now?

ELLA. Because Danny didn't feel like talking this over with his dad. I told him that he owed you that much.

1

SOL. Well, where is he now?

ELLA. Search me, Sol. He's put our entire life savings into starting a nightclub with his sleazy friend Terrence. They're gonna call it "Mad Money." I call it "My Money."

SOL. How could this happen?

ELLA. It just did.

SOL. He's got his Masters from Columbia, for God's sake!

ELLA. What the fuck does that have to do with anything?

SOL. I just don't understand how this happened.

ELLA. I blame you, Sol.

SOL. Me?

ELLA. Yeah. You. Danny doesn't know who he is, because you never helped him find out. All that terrible stuff with his mom –

SOL. What do you know about it?

ELLA. I don't know anything, "Dad." And neither does Danny. Because you keep everything buried. That's what you taught him, how to bury the past.

You screwed him up really good. I hope you're proud of yourself.

SOL. That's not fair! He's not a kid. He's a grown man now.

ELLA. I wish.

> (**ELLA** *exits.* **SOL** *closes the door, looks out, processing.*)

SOL. Danny.

> (*Spot rises on* **DANNY**, *a forty-year-old bi-racial man, dressed nicely, like the inner-city high school teacher he was. He is a mirage here,* **SOL**'s *illusion.* **SOL** *approaches him, but the spot goes down on* **DANNY**, *who exits.*)

(Speaks to the webcam. When he does so, his image is projected on the pre-set monitor.) I tried to reach you, Danny, I did, but you were gone, and you weren't returning my messages. So I clapped my noise-canceling headphones back on my head and turned up Miles Davis. Miles said that the secret of life is forgetting: People. Places. Events. But most of all people. "You can't hear the licks if you got all those names in your head," Miles said. But soon I got this idea in my head, and then Miles wasn't working anymore. If I could just make some recordings, and then give you the tapes... the truth about what really happened with me and your mom! ...Maybe then you would understand me. And you could forgive me. And love me again.

> *(Spot up on **FRANK SLEZAK**, a Newark PD detective.)*

SLEZAK. Don't even try, Eisner. You're not up to the task.

SOL. Cal?

> *(Spot up also on **CALVIN JAMES**, thirty-five, a heavyweight boxer in a robe that has the name "SAVAGE" stenciled on the back.)*

CALVIN. I'm the only one that's got the truth, an' it has to be spoken!

> *(**CALVIN** tosses off his robe and shadow-boxes. He stops and smiles, nodding, raising his arms, certain that he just knocked out his opponent.)*

> *(**CAL** and **SOL** make eye contact. **CAL**'s stare puts a scare in **SOL**.)*

> *(Spot up also on **ADELE SPARKS**, thirty-three, who looks at **SOL**, smiling.)*

ADELE. What about me, baby? You gonna take me on too?

(**SOL** *looks away, unable to look at her.*)

(*Lights down on Sol's apartment, rise at half-level on a jail cell in Essex County lockup, 1978.*)

LUGO. *(In a jail cell in semi-darkness.)* Smoke?

YOUNG SOL. What?

LUGO. Got a smoke?

YOUNG SOL. You Jimmy Lugo?

LUGO. You got a smoke?

YOUNG SOL. Sorry.

      (**LUGO** *curses.*)

What's the idea here? No guards? And they just leave your cell door open?

LUGO. What's a' matter? You scared? It's County. No one gives a shit.

YOUNG SOL. You're a hard man to find, Mr. Lugo.

LUGO. So who's looking for me?

YOUNG SOL. Sol Eisner. *Newark Star-Ledger*. Working on the Savage James case.

LUGO. What, that old thing?

YOUNG SOL. Your testimony put him away.

LUGO. That's old news.

YOUNG SOL. Now you testified under oath, Mr. Lugo, that you were pulling a warehouse heist at Zodiac Storage on the night of July 17, 1971 –

LUGO. "Put him away." That's right, I put him away. Joe Frazier couldn't do it, Jimmy Ellis couldn't, Floyd fucking Patterson couldn't, but I did. Jimmy Lugo. *(He snickers.)*

YOUNG SOL. *(Takes out his tape recorder, turns it on.)* You said that – in the middle of the robbery – you just happened to look out the window that gave on to the alley –

LUGO. *(Motions to turn off recorder.)* You got a smoke? 'Cause you wouldn't get in trouble or nothing if you gave me one.

YOUNG SOL. Now, Mr. Lugo...

LUGO. Turn that thing off.

YOUNG SOL. Why?

> *(**LUGO** motions: **YOUNG SOL** turns off the recorder.)*

LUGO. You wanna know the truth? I'll tell you the truth.

YOUNG SOL. Just like that?

> *(**LUGO** shrugs. **YOUNG SOL** presses "record.")*

LUGO. You got twenty dollars?

YOUNG SOL. *(Turns off the recorder.)* Lugo...

LUGO. I could buy a lotta smokes for twenty dollars.

YOUNG SOL. You think I'm that dumb? Guard! Guard!

LUGO. Just slip it to me. Come on. I won't tell.

COUNTY GUARD. *(Enters.)* You ready?

YOUNG SOL. I want to put this twenty dollars into Mr. Lugo's account. It's a loan, you understand, which he's going to pay me back later.

COUNTY GUARD. *(Takes money.)* Hurry up, I'm watching the game. *(Exits.)*

LUGO. What the fuck you do that for? Now I'll never get it.

YOUNG SOL. Don't worry, it's in your account.

LUGO. You know what these fucks do? They beat me up every night, just for kicks.

 (Pulls up his shirt.)

YOUNG SOL. You want to get back at them? Then start talking... *(He presses "record.")*

 *(Lights down on **LUGO**, rise on **DETECTIVE SLEZAK** at his desk at Police HQ. **YOUNG SOL** sits, facing him.)*

SLEZAK. I'm perfectly aware that you hate me. That your whole generation hates me. And – to be perfectly honest – I hate them. But that doesn't mean there has to be any bad feelings between us. On a personal level, I mean.

YOUNG SOL. I'm just a reporter, Detective.

SLEZAK. Right.

YOUNG SOL. Trying to get all the facts.

SLEZAK. Okay. Let's look at the facts.

 (Opens a folder, looks at rap sheet.)

Calvin James: first arrested for robbery at seven years old. In and out of juvenile homes until fifteen, when he escapes with another boy. Both picked up two months later for armed robbery.

YOUNG SOL. Look, I'm already aware of this –

SLEZAK. Arrested for assault and battery at eighteen. Picked up on another assault charge fifteen months later.

YOUNG SOL. Which was dropped.

SLEZAK. I'll skip over the minor offenses...

YOUNG SOL. This is ancient history.

SLEZAK. The guy is *bad*, don't you see? He's rotten. He started out rotten, he did rotten things, until finally one day he exploded.

YOUNG SOL. You left out how he turned himself around in prison and should have been heavyweight champ.

SLEZAK. Which is exactly why he did these murders!

YOUNG SOL. What?

SLEZAK. James is waiting for his shot at Ali, right? Finally he gets it. But two months before, Ali's stripped of his title by the Commission. Meanwhile, the riots go down, his friends are killed, his neighborhood wiped out. Then one night Calvin James sees this nice Jewish couple, a little sloshed, in a place where they shouldn't be. And he –

YOUNG SOL. Why tell me? Do I look like a jury?

SLEZAK. I feel for you, kid.

YOUNG SOL. Why?

SLEZAK. I don't know, I was young once, I believed in stupid things. I'm trying to wisen you up.

YOUNG SOL. When people find out that Savage was framed –

SLEZAK. Uh-huh. So much for an open-minded look at the facts.

YOUNG SOL. How about giving me a look at that folder?

SLEZAK. Right.

YOUNG SOL. I thought you had nothing to hide?

SLEZAK. Do your own homework. You can't copy mine.

> (**SLEZAK** *smiles, takes out a key on a chain, opens a file cabinet drawer.* **YOUNG SOL** *promptly raises his right hand, waves it around;* **ROOKS** *enters. The scene freezes,*

focus returns to **SOL** *in Brooklyn 2020, speaking to* **DANNY** *through the webcam.)*

SOL. Oh, so I should have told you, Danny, I had developed this source inside the Newark PD who was as disgusted with all the corruption as I was. His name was Danny too. Danny Rooks. And what happened next was a slick move that we had set up.

(**ROOKS**, *a desk cop, enters and goes to* **SLEZAK**.)

ROOKS. Uh, Detective?

SLEZAK. Yeah?

ROOKS. Just thought you should know: Sergeant Johnson is moving that desk again.

SLEZAK. What?

ROOKS. Yeah. And he says, uh, that you can go fuck yourself.

SLEZAK. Does he? Well, fuck him.

(**SLEZAK** *storms out, followed by* **ROOKS**. **YOUNG SOL** *opens the drawer, removes the tape, stuffs it in his briefcase, and exits.)*

(*We see the following interrogation in a shadow-filled half-light:)*

So you looked out the winda and what did you see?

LUGO. I don't know. It was dark.

SLEZAK. Fact is, Lugo, I got my hand so far up your ass, I can feel your little heart beating. And if you don't start bein' a little more cooperative here, this could get messy. So you looked out the winda and you saw what?

LUGO. A middle-aged white couple and a Black guy.

SLEZAK. So you had a good view of the scene, right? You could see it real clearly?

LUGO. Oh yeah. Man had on a polo shirt, light-colored, with one of them little alligators on it – you know, what's that brand...shit...with that cute little alligator with its jaws open?

SLEZAK. Who gives a shit?!

*(Lights fade on **LUGO** and **SLEZAK**, who exit.)*

*(Lights rise on **SOL** in Brooklyn again, in front of the webcam.)*

SOL. I went to your home last week to see JJ. Your son really misses you, Danny. He's only nine years old, for God's sake, and you'll never get this time with him again.

*(Lights fade on Sol's apartment, rise on a cellblock room in Trenton State Prison, February 1978. **TYRONE BELL** [in prison garb] addresses **YOUNG SOL** and **ADELE SPARKS**, a Black community activist, and **RAY BRANIFF**, thirty-five, a white radical. Behind them lounges a **GUARD** and **CALVIN** in a prison jumpsuit.)*

TYRONE. Now I just gotta say somethin' 'bout this brother... All the brothers say they not guilty, but Calvin *is*. He's the most not guilty man ever *was*. You hear me?

ADELE. You tell it, brother Tyrone! Shout it from the rooftops so the blind can see and the deaf can hear!

RAY. Yeah! Absolutely! Let 'em have it right between the eyes!

TYRONE. That's why we here, ain't it? To keep the ball rollin' that Brother Sol started with his front page in-your-face headlines. You are the most truth-telling white man I ever run into, Brother Sol, and I ain't ashamed to say I pegged you all wrong.

(He and **YOUNG SOL** *shake hands.* **ADELE** *and* **RAY** *applaud.)*

YOUNG SOL. Look – I'm a reporter, okay? I can't be a member of any committee and still –

TYRONE. We unnerstand, Brother Sol. You here in the interest of Justice, right? Well, so are we.

YOUNG SOL. But I can't be an advocate for any cause.

RAY. What happened to staying true to your underground roots, man? You sounding awfully mainstream.

ADELE. *(To* **RAY.***)* For your information, we *need* mainstream. He has the access, and we don't.

RAY. Absolutely. All I'm sayin' is –

TYRONE. Ray Braniff, we welcome your 'sperience with organizin'. And Miss Adele Sparks – I can't tell you how much it means to have a woman o' your standin' in the neighborhoods here...

CALVIN. *(In background.)* Hey Youngblood: how 'bout I tell 'em myself?

> *(***TYRONE** *sits among* **ADELE, RAY,** *and* **YOUNG SOL,** *as* **CALVIN JAMES** *comes down front:)*
>
> *(He is physically powerful, yet the dominant impression he makes is of a once-violent man who has disciplined his rage. He wears gold wire-rimmed glasses that contrast with his athletic appearance.)*

(To **TYRONE.***)* And to think I thought you was the quiet type. *(Pause.)* I been waitin' on this day a long time. A *long* time. Six years, four months and twenty-three days. And eleven hours and forty-six minutes. *(Looks at his watch.)* Make that forty-seven minutes. And that's not counting the time I spent in lock-up before the trial, or all them other trumped-up charges they hauled

me in on before they found somethin' they could make stick. And man, did they find somethin'.

RAY. We know it's bullshit! We're with you! It's out in the open now! Look what happened to Nixon!

CALVIN. Nixon ain't servin' no time. Calvin James is. That's the difference.

RAY. But "truth will out." That's my point.

CALVIN. Nixon be home with his family, eatin' turkey and gravy. I look around and I don't see no Nixon. I'm here. *(Looks at his watch.)* Fifty-one minutes. *(Pause.)* I done time before. It goes slow, but I could handle it 'cause I was guilty. But every second that passes by now…

RAY. Oh *man*. You wanna start planning some actions? Right on! Let's smash a pie in Slezak's face or chain ourselves to a fence. But cut the Timex bullshit, okay? Very uncool.

ADELE. Talk about *uncool*. Nobody wanna hear you flappin' your lips with your old radical bullshit.

RAY. I'm waitin' to hear something. C'mon. *(Pause.)* Huey P. Newton. Bobby Seale. Soledad Brother George Jackson. They took a stand and paid the price. I know who they are, what they stood for. Who are you, Mr. Timex?

TYRONE. *(Stands; to CALVIN.)* What did I tell you about him?

CALVIN. Tyrone.

(Pause, then TYRONE sits.)

(To RAY.) Don't you be talkin' no George Jackson here. I aim to walk outta this snake pit on my own power, a free man.

RAY. Sounds to me like he was a freer man dead than you are alive.

TYRONE. Okay, cracker. That's it.

(*He comes at* **RAY**. *The* **GUARD** *intervenes.*)

PRISON GUARD. (*To* **TYRONE**.) Control that temper, Mister. (*To everyone.*) This meeting is over!

CALVIN. (*To* **GUARD**.) It's okay, Joe. I'll handle it.

PRISON GUARD. Well, there better not be any more outbursts. (*He retreats upstage.*)

RAY. Sorry I flew off the handle. We're all on the same side here.

TYRONE. No, sir, Calvin. He's gotta go.

RAY. I said I was sorry. Let's get on with it.

TYRONE. I'm tellin' you, Calvin. He's gonna turn. You know that I'm right.

RAY. (*To* **TYRONE**.) Fuck you. I came here of my own free will, because I believe in something. You're just a convict who steals purses from old ladies.

CALVIN. Goodbye, Mister Braniff.

RAY. Hey Calvin, come on. You *need* me. I'm your grassroots guy. If you're gonna get your word out to the people –

CALVIN. Goodbye.

TYRONE. You heard the man. Move it.

RAY. Okay... I'll remember this when we take over...

(**RAY** *exits.* **TYRONE** *and* **CAL** *confer off to the side.*)

ADELE. (*To* **YOUNG SOL**.) Oh, I hate to see things like that.

YOUNG SOL. Yeah, that's really messed up. I'm Sol.

ADELE. Adele. Hey.

YOUNG SOL. Hey.

ADELE. Hey.

YOUNG SOL. I've heard a lot of good things about your work in the schools…

ADELE. Have you?

YOUNG SOL. But something like this – It's gonna take a lot of people working together.

ADELE. I hope that means you too. You write so well.

YOUNG SOL. But it's people like you who are making the real difference.

ADELE. You think so?

YOUNG SOL. Oh yeah. That's how things get changed.

ADELE. Why, thank you so much, Sol.

*(Pause: They stop and look at **CAL**.)*

CALVIN. Hey, just go on talkin'. I got nowhere to go, except to a five-by-nine cell. *(Looks at his watch.)* Twelve hours and ten minutes.

ADELE. At the risk of sounding like Ray: What's our plan?

GUARD. Two minutes.

CALVIN. What?

GUARD. You got two minutes more. *(He turns away.)*

CALVIN. *(To **ADELE**.)* You gonna be my spokesman.

ADELE. You mean "spokes*woman*."

CALVIN. You gonna be spreading the word in the Black community and the Black press.

ADELE. So I can't speak to white people? Why's that?

YOUNG SOL. I think she has a point.

CALVIN. *(To **SOL**.)* We gotta talk.

ADELE. Why you talkin' with him and not me?

CALVIN. *(Drops a large manilla envelope on the table.)*
This is my story. The one hundred percent truth. Make
sure it gets published.

YOUNG SOL. I can't believe what I'm hearing.

CALVIN. You in the writing business, right?

YOUNG SOL. I'm in the reporting business. It's different.

CALVIN. It's gotta be out in the stores in three months.

YOUNG SOL. Impossible. Things don't happen that quickly.
It takes a year –

CALVIN. I don't have it.

ADELE. What do you mean? Who's after you?

CALVIN. Ask Tyrone.

TYRONE. There are dark forces at work.

ADELE. What kind of forces?

TYRONE. Who do you think? Who's been killin' all the
strong Black men?

YOUNG SOL. What're you talking about?

ADELE. Yeah. Just come out and say it.

CALVIN. Three months! Don't let me down!

       (Lights down on the prison.)

       *(Lights rise on **ADELE** and **YOUNG SOL** at a
       bar at the train station.)*

YOUNG SOL. So what convinced you that Savage was
innocent?

ADELE. Have you seen the man box? He's got pride. That's
not a man who would ever kill an old couple!

YOUNG SOL. Some people think he just hates white people.

ADELE. Sol. Don't be talking such nonsense to me.

YOUNG SOL. Then tell me why you think he's not guilty.

ADELE. Well... I saw the man tell the truth in front of the world!

YOUNG SOL. You mean after that fight?

ADELE. Oh yeah! I will never ever forget it!

> *(Lights up on boxing arena, 1967.* **TV ANNOUNCER**, *with* **CAL** *in his "Savage" robe and* **BERNARD**, *his trainer.)*

ANNOUNCER. Wrapping this up now, from the Arena in Atlantic City –

SAVAGE. Hold on a minute.

ANNOUNCER. You have something else to say, Savage?

SAVAGE. Yeah. About those riots goin' down now in Newark and Patterson –

BERNARD. No, Savage! *(To the camera.)* No comment!

SAVAGE. *(Pushes him aside.)* What I did to Bobby Gannon tonight – that's what's gonna happen to all you white people, if you don't learn how to treat folks! And that's a promise.

ANNOUNCER. Are you really advocating violence?

SAVAGE. I'm sayin' just what it sounds like. So y'all better wake up out there, before it's too late. We're people too! And we ain't gonna let this go on!

> *(Lights down on the boxing arena, stay up on* **YOUNG SOL** *and* **ADELE**.*)*

YOUNG SOL. Yeah, I remember. My dad was dying of cancer.

ADELE. Oh, I'm so sorry, baby.

YOUNG SOL. We were watching in his hospital room, and when that happened – "That man just signed his death warrant," he said.

ADELE. So that's what convinced you? That he was innocent, I mean.

YOUNG SOL. I don't know. He was my dad's favorite fighter. I just couldn't take it if he was guilty.

> *(Lights down on* **YOUNG SOL** *and* **ADELE,** *rise on* **CAL** *at a prison table.)*

> *(The* **GUARD** *listens to the radio.* **YOUNG SOL** *enters with a briefcase.)*

CALVIN. Hey, my man. You got it?

> *(***YOUNG SOL** *places a book in front of* **CALVIN.***)*

Ha-ha! *(Picks up book.)* And you said no way to three months! You got to think *positive*, brother, you hear me?

YOUNG SOL. Yeah, amazing how fast people move to exploit a hot story.

CALVIN. And who made it hot, brother? Who? *(Pause: gazes at book.)* "The Savage Fight." Ain't it the truth? 'Cause I been fightin' since the day I was born, my moms say I came out kickin' an' screamin', like I was pissed off and was gonna make somebody pay.

YOUNG SOL. Yeah, I read the book.

CALVIN. You did more than that, brother! All them years slavin' away, puttin' one word 'n front of 'nother, this voice in my head sayin', "What you doin' now, fool?" An' then you come along out a nowhere, an' you expose all them lies been done to me, an' fix up my book one two three, make it sound like I gone to Harvard or somethin'.

YOUNG SOL. You were lucky to get a good editor.

CALVIN. And who got 'im for me? Huh? Who?

YOUNG SOL. Look, Cal, I didn't do anything special.

CALVIN. But you did, brother. You did. You had *faith*.

YOUNG SOL. I'm sure you would've done the same for me, if you thought I was given a raw deal.

CALVIN. The man I am now maybe, but Savage – Savage woulda *laughed* at you, brother, he woulda *hooted*. "Now the white boy find out what it feels like to be a nigger," he woulda snapped.

YOUNG SOL. Wasn't it Savage who stuck his neck out on nationwide TV? Wasn't it Savage who told J. Edgar Hoover "fuck you"?

CALVIN. Man, you smart in some ways, but in others… I'm gonna let you in on a secret, bro: Savage James wuz a beast, a damn animal, much worse than I ev'n let on in here – *(Points to book.)* 'Course it wasn't completely his fault, but take my word: you woulda stood in his way, he woulda broke you like candy 'n sucked on your bones.

YOUNG SOL. I know what I saw… You really believed in something. You put yourself out there.

CALVIN. What you saw, brother, was a freak, an illusion. So happens my trainer, Bernie – his half-sister Hazel had some kinda shop in Harlem, some bo-tique or somethin', an' he was goin' on and on 'bout how them white cops were cheerin' the looters an' all. The man got on my nerves, talkin' like that before a big fight, so I says either *do* somethin' 'bout it or shut the fuck up! But Bernie, he keeps goin' on, so I opens my big mouth on coast-to-coast TV to teach 'im a lesson. Now I ask you, brother Sol, sittin' here ten years later: who was it got taught the lesson?

YOUNG SOL. Are you fucking with me now, or is that really the truth?

CALVIN. Swear to God. An' Calvin does not do that lightly.

YOUNG SOL. That's not what you wrote in the book.

CALVIN. You crazy, man! I wanna get outta here! You and Tyrone the only ones know. Except Bernie, of course...

YOUNG SOL. You lied to me.

CALVIN. I just re-interpreted the truth a little, brother. It happens all the time.

YOUNG SOL. I put my reputation on the line! I vouched for the absolute truthfulness of every word in your book. Now you're telling me that you were pissed at your trainer, not at any injustice.

CALVIN. Hey, Tyrone ain't gonna tell anyone. An' Bernie, hey, he's an ol' man.

YOUNG SOL. Why do you think you can trust me? I'm a reporter. In fact, that's what I came here to say. Now that the book's coming out, and it looks like Maxie Laszlo's going to do your PR –

CALVIN. Maxie Laszlo? The guy who elected the governor?

YOUNG SOL. The point is, you don't need me. Not like before.

CALVIN. Oh. So it's like that...

YOUNG SOL. I just think that it would be better for everyone –

CALVIN. I shoulda known better. You see, Savage, he was so suspicious, he wouldn't tell nobody nothin', but *Calvin* –

YOUNG SOL. Look, I'll honor your confidence.

CALVIN. *(Picks up book.)* Wish to hell my daddy coulda seen this. Goddamn! He never thought I'd amount to nothin'. Even when I stood toe-to-toe with Smokin' Joe Frazier –

YOUNG SOL. Stop changing the subject.

CALVIN. Ya know, my brother Harold, he got his Masters in Engineerin'. Peoples don' know that 'bout me, think I come from trash. I guess they'll know better now...

> *(Suddenly adopts a "slave" accent.)*

An' it all thanks to you, Massa Sol! You done bust yo' little behind for little ol' Calvin, an' he be so thankf'l, Massa, he be tellin' de lord 'bout all de charity you be doin'!

YOUNG SOL. Stop it!

CALVIN. Oh Lordy, Lordy, lay up a treasure for Massa 'n heav'n, cuz he be earning it tenfold down here!

YOUNG SOL. Shut the fuck up!

> *(***YOUNG SOL*** *reaches across and pushes* **CALVIN.***)*

PRISON GUARD. *(Jumps up.)* Hey, did you push him? There's no contact allowed here. That's physical assault, Mister. *(To* **CAL.***)* Did he push you?

> *(Pause: then* **CALVIN** *laughs, a deep rumbling laugh that won't stop.)*

What's so funny?

CALVIN. Who am I, Joe?

PRISON GUARD. Savage James.

CALVIN. What did I do for a living? I made a pretty good living, didn't I? How many people have put their hands on me and lived to tell about it?

> *(***GUARD*** *laughs.* **CALVIN** *laughs.* **GUARD** *sits back down.)*

I wouldn't try that again.

YOUNG SOL. Right.

CALVIN. I may not be Savage anymore, but even Calvin has a pretty fair jab.

YOUNG SOL. I hope you saw my point too though.

CALVIN. The only point, brother Sol, is that if you start something, you gotta have the guts to go all the way.

YOUNG SOL. And that's what I'm trying to do.

CALVIN. You gotta keep fightin' and fightin' 'til that other mutherfucker goes down, or 'til the bell rings, an' it's in the hands o' the judges.

YOUNG SOL. But I never said –

CALVIN. You came to me from the outside, you fought for Calvin when Calvin couldn't fight for hisself. We halfway there, brother! You gonna keep fightin' beside me or you gonna take the glory and run?

(Lights fade on prison cell.)

Scene Two

(October 1978, the press conference for **CAL**'*s release from prison – in the dark: one pin spotlight picks up the black satin boxing robe with the word "SAVAGE" stenciled in large white letters on the back, as it dangles by a wire from the ceiling, seemingly floating.)*

STENTORIAN VOICE. *(Voice-over.)* For the last eight years Calvin James has languished in prison for a crime he did not commit. Thus was one of the great sports careers of our era cut off in its prime.

(The robe is slowly hoisted out of view.)

But Calvin the man has fought to clear his name, and last month his titanic struggles finally paid off! *(Applause.)* Ladies and Gentlemen – Calvin James!

(Pin spot fades, a stark spot picks up **CALVIN** *at the podium.)*

CALVIN. Man, if you knew how many nights I stayed up picturing this day in my mind – and now here it is. And there you are. And sweet freedom, you're here too. Ha-ha! But even as I give thanks to the lord and to all my good friends for gettin' me a new trial, I have to ask: why was I here in the first place? What was my crime? Not killing some nice married couple who drove in from the suburbs to see some colored people up close. No! Not even Hoover himself, in his wildest wet dream, could have believed that. I was gonna be the Champeen, everyone knew, Champeen of the whole goddamn world! Why would I go out and shoot these poor people who never did nothing to me? Please! It boggles the mind, defies any logic. No, I been locked up for one reason and one reason only: I spoke the truth. And on nationwide coast-to-coast TV no less! And the best way to silence the truth is to lock up or kill the person who speaks it. So all these years later, here I am, brothers and sisters, still fightin' for my freedom with two hands, still refusin' to take a dive. And do you think I'm gonna stop now? Hell no!

ADELE. *(Stands, responds from audience.)* Hell no!

CALVIN. Hell no!

ADELE. Hell no!

CALVIN. Hell no!

ADELE. Hell no! Hell no! Hell no!

> *(Others chant "Hell no!" as* **CALVIN** *raises his arms in a victory pose.)*

> *(Stark spot fades into general lighting for the reception:)*

> *(People surround* **CAL**, *talking, holding drinks.)*

> *(***YOUNG SOL** *and* **ADELE** *are downstage right, by themselves.)*

YOUNG SOL. Hey, that was something. Did you two have that planned out?

ADELE. What?

YOUNG SOL. You know – the chant.

ADELE. I was moved. Okay? The man moved me.

YOUNG SOL. Uh-huh. So what do you say, Adele?

ADELE. Sol... Let's go back to the party.

YOUNG SOL. You heard Maxie. They'll probably put Calvin's face on a box of Wheaties. Look, Adele. I feel something for you. Something that I've never felt –

ADELE. Sol, don't –

YOUNG SOL. I have to.

ADELE. You couldn't handle it, baby. Believe me.

YOUNG SOL. I'd sure like to give it the old college try.

ADELE. You really feel that much for me, baby? You think you understand me?

YOUNG SOL. You're just like me, Adele. We're great helping others, but when it comes to ourselves...we just screw it up.

ADELE. You're right about that.

YOUNG SOL. I'm right about lots of things, Adele. Just give me a chance to show you.

> (**YOUNG SOL** *pulls* **ADELE** *closer, kisses her.*)

ADELE. You're not gonna hurt me, baby, are you?

> (*They kiss again. There is a knock on the door of Sol's apartment in the present. Lights down suddenly on* **YOUNG SOL** *and* **ADELE**.)

> (**SOL** *in his sixties opens his apartment door in the middle of the night.* **DANNY** *enters with* **TINA**, *an aging party girl; her clothes are very shiny.*)

DANNY. *(Dressed slick, very tipsy.)* Hey Pops.

SOL. Danny? Do you know what time it is?

DANNY. Pops, this is Tina. Tina, this is Pops.

TINA. *(Also tipsy.)* Hey Pops!

> (**TINA** *kisses* **SOL** *on the mouth.*)

SOL. Please call me "Sol."

TINA. Okay "Soul."

SOL. No, "Sol." Say it. "Sol."

TINA. You have something to drink, Soul?

SOL. Sorry, I don't.

DANNY. I know where there's some vodka.

SOL. No, Danny, don't – Please –

> (**DANNY** *exits into the offstage kitchen.*)
>
> (**SOL** *is left alone with* **TINA.** *He is clearly ill at ease.*)

TINA. You're cute.

SOL. No. I'm not.

TINA. You're a really good person then. I have a good feeling about you.

SOL. Look, Tina, it's late, and I'm really – [tired]

> (**DANNY** *re-enters with three shot glasses brimming with vodka.*)

DANNY. Here we go! Instant party!

TINA. Yay!

> (*She takes a glass.* **SOL** *reluctantly takes a glass too.*)

SOL. Danny, we need to talk.

DANNY. (*Raises his glass.*) Here's to warm bodies on a cold night – and all the wonderful things they can do!

> (**DANNY** *downs his drink in one gulp.*)

TINA. Yay!

> (**TINA** *downs her drink in one gulp too.*)

SOL. Danny! Please! We have things to talk about! Important things!

TINA. Come on, Soul.

SOL. You quit your job, you leave your wife and child, and I don't even get a phone call? You expect me to celebrate that?

DANNY. *(To* SOL.*)* We can't all be one of a kind.

TINA. Well I am!

DANNY. That's right! Good for you!

> (DANNY *slaps her on the butt. She laughs. He heads for the door.)*

SOL. Danny, I'm worried about you. Really worried. Where are you going?

DANNY. Have fun, Pops. You'll never get this time with her again.

SOL. What? No!

DANNY. La Dolce Vita! Arrivederci Roma!

SOL. Danny, come back here! I'm ordering you to come back and talk with me!

> (DANNY *exits. Pause.* SOL *walks back inside, sits, forgets* TINA *is there.)*

TINA. Hi Soul.

SOL. Sorry. You can let yourself out.

> (He exits to his bedroom, closes the door. TINA *sighs, pours herself another drink, sits, sips. Lights down on this scene, rise on* SLEZAK *in a diner, eating a burger and fries, drinking a Coke.)*

SLEZAK. So you really think you can win this thing, huh? Just beat me straight out in court?

> (Shakes his head, resumes eating.)

SLEZAK. Don't just stand there. Come on over. I'm not gonna bite you, okay?

(**YOUNG SOL** *is still offstage.*)

You see, I'm not afraid to come out in public, no matter what they say about me.

YOUNG SOL. *(Enters.)* Why did I have to come here?

SLEZAK. Hey, what's the big deal? The worst that happens, you get a free meal. *(Calls out.)* Polly! Hey Polly!

(**WAITRESS** *enters.*)

Our friend here wants something to eat.

WAITRESS. *(To* **SOL.***)* You comin' or goin'? I don't got all day.

YOUNG SOL. *(Sits.)* Just a coffee and a rice pudding.

WAITRESS. Good choice. *(Exits.)*

YOUNG SOL. So what's the big idea, Slezak? I'm busy.

SLEZAK. Yeah, smearing my good name.

YOUNG SOL. Hey, if the alligator shirt fits...

SLEZAK. Why make this so personal? I'm a sensitive guy, you know.

YOUNG SOL. Right.

WAITRESS. *(Enters with dishes.)* Coffee and a rice pudding. *(Puts down dishes on table.)*

(To **YOUNG SOL.***)* Hey, you're kinda cute. You got a girlfriend?

YOUNG SOL. No. I've been saving myself for you.

WAITRESS. Fresh. *(Exits.)*

SLEZAK. So this is how I see it: you got Lugo's recantation, which is worth less than shit, since everyone knows he's the world's biggest liar.

YOUNG SOL. *(Eats pudding.)* Did you have her put something in this? It tastes... *(Pushes it away.)*

SLEZAK. You got the police stoppin' some other cars, and people sayin' they're "not sure" if the taillights matched Savage's car – but they might have. And that's basically it. Nothing but smokescreen.

YOUNG SOL. You seem to be choking on it.

SLEZAK. Hey, I got a wife and two kids. They hear things in school.

YOUNG SOL. Calvin had a wife and two kids too.

SLEZAK. Yeah, a real family man.

> *(**YOUNG SOL** shrugs and gets up to leave.)*

You tell that Madison Avenue sleaze to lay off me, if he knows what's good for him.

YOUNG SOL. It's been a real pleasure.

> *(**YOUNG SOL** exits.)*

SLEZAK. *(Yells after him.)* I'm gonna kick your New York tails, Eisner! I'm gonna take on the whole goddamn media, and I'm gonna win!

> *(Lights down on **SLEZAK.**)*

> *(Lights rise on **YOUNG SOL** and **ADELE** under the covers, January 1979.)*

ADELE. You're really passionate.

YOUNG SOL. Don't sound so surprised.

ADELE. Well, I am a little...

YOUNG SOL. Why? Because I'm white?

ADELE. No. Because you're smart.

YOUNG SOL. Smart enough to know what a prize you are.

(He kisses her.)

(They break apart. **ADELE** *has a half-smile, half-frown.)*

YOUNG SOL. What?

ADELE. You really think this could go anywhere, Sol?

YOUNG SOL. It already has.

ADELE. Oh, so that's all you wanted? A few rolls in the hay?

YOUNG SOL. I want everything, Adele. Everything. And I want it with you.

ADELE. I just don't know if I have it to give, baby.

YOUNG SOL. To me, you mean?

ADELE. I just don't know.

*(***YOUNG SOL** *pulls away.)*

Don't be like that, baby. I really feel something for you.

YOUNG SOL. *(Turns back to her.)* You do?

ADELE. I want this to work, baby.

YOUNG SOL. It has to. You're everything I've ever wanted, Adele. I'm crazy about you.

ADELE. Are you, baby? Are you really?

(Phone rings in Young Sol's apartment. **ADELE** *indicates he should pick it up.)*

YOUNG SOL. *(Answers phone.)* Yeah?

TYRONE. *(At prison pay phone.)* Hey Brother Sol! What's the good word?

YOUNG SOL. Who's this?

TYRONE. What's a' matta, bro? Don't you reckonize Calvin's right hand? *(Laughs.)* Y'all runnin' 'round havin' a good time, while poor Tyrone's just doin' time.

YOUNG SOL. Something I can help you with, Tyrone?

TYRONE. I'm just checkin' in, Brother Sol. How's it goin'? How's Calvin?

YOUNG SOL. He's busy getting ready for the retrial.

TYRONE. Well, that's what I'm callin' about! Let's get all the brothers together out here!

YOUNG SOL. I don't think that's a good idea.

TYRONE. Why not? Is Calvin too good now to hang with the brothers?

YOUNG SOL. I've got to go now, Tyrone.

TYRONE. Oh do you, Brother Sol? What if I told you that Calvin's been playin' you for a sucker.

YOUNG SOL. Bullshit!

TYRONE. We both have! Ha ha! He's guilty as hell, man! Guilty as hell!

> (**TYRONE** *laughs.* **YOUNG SOL** *slams the phone down.*)
>
> (*Light down on* **TYRONE**.)

ADELE. What? What is it?

> (**YOUNG SOL** *shakes his head.*)

Is it Calvin? He's not hurt, is he?

> (**YOUNG SOL** *shakes his head.*)

Well, thank God for that.

YOUNG SOL. You don't have any doubts about Calvin, do you?

ADELE. Why? Should I?

YOUNG SOL. You tell me.

> *(Spot up on* **CALVIN** *at one part of the stage.)*
>
> *(Spot up on* **SOL** *in his Park Slope apartment, in front of his webcam.)*
>
> *(And spot up on* **DANNY,** *who wears sunglasses, smokes a joint.)*
>
> *(Lights fade on* **YOUNG SOL** *and* **ADELE.** *Then spotlight down on* **CALVIN,** *too.)*
>
> *(Lights remain for a few moments on* **SOL** *and* **DANNY.***)*
>
> *(***DANNY** *takes a deep toke, then exhales a plume of smoke. He stubs out the joint, pockets it, and walks offstage, leaving behind the empty pool of light.)*
>
> *(***SOL** *takes a deep, worry-filled breath, then lets it out with a sigh, shaking his head.)*
>
> *(Then both spots fade to darkness.)*

Intermission

ACT II

*(Lights up on **SOL** in January 2020, speaking to the webcam. As always when he's there, his image is projected up on the monitor.)*

SOL. Are you watching my videotapes, Danny? Are you listening?

I've been dropping the tapes off with Ella when I bring JJ those little tangerines that he loves. But none of it makes any sense unless you watch them. The things that happened – I don't know if I can explain them so you'll understand. Then again, I'm not sure that I understand, even now.

Sometimes I lie awake at night, and this feeling comes over me: if I can just put the past in a package and give it to Danny, maybe it will be like a small sun, a source of heat and warmth, that will melt this iceberg between us...

*(Spot up on **ADELE** on hotel phone.)*

ADELE. *(Into phone.)* Hello Sol? Yeah baby, it's me.

SOL. *(From the present – looks at his memory of **ADELE**, shaking his head.)* No.

ADELE. *(Into phone.)* Hello Sol? Yeah baby, it's me.

SOL. I don't want to remember this.

ADELE. *(Into phone.)* Hello Sol? Yeah baby, it's me.

SOL. Do something, Miles! Do something!

(A blast of hard-edged Miles Davis jazz plays.)*

(The spot on **ADELE** *remains.)*

(Another blast of Miles.)*

ADELE. *(Into phone.)* Hello Sol? Yeah baby, it's me.

    *(***SOL*** *screams, storms offstage. Lights down on* **ADELE.***)*

    (Lights rise on **SLEZAK** *at his desk, looking over some paperwork.)*

    *(***YOUNG SOL*** *bursts in, followed by a* **POLICEWOMAN.***)*

YOUNG SOL. You bastard!

POLICEWOMAN. *(Grabs hold of* **YOUNG SOL.***)* Sorry, sir. He ran by me.

SLEZAK. It's okay. No harm done.

    (To **POLICEWOMAN.***)* You can let go of him.

POLICEWOMAN. *(Lets go.)* You want me to stay, sir?

    *(***SLEZAK** *shakes his head. She exits.)*

SLEZAK. Always a pleasure to see you, Sol.

YOUNG SOL. Don't pull that smug act with me.

SLEZAK. *(Leans back.)* So what's on your mind?

YOUNG SOL. You've been tampering with our defense witness, Belinda Clark.

SLEZAK. So you know where she is?

---

*A license to produce *Savage World* does not include a performance license for any third-party or copyrighted music. Licensees should create an original composition or use music in the public domain. For further information, please see the Music and Third-Party Materials Use Note on page iii.

YOUNG SOL. Or should I say "Karen Rubins"?

SLEZAK. I don't know. Should you?

YOUNG SOL. You've been moving her from house to house. That's a felony.

SLEZAK. Have any proof? Right. Just like you got nothin' to exonerate James.

What you do have is trouble for making a threat against an Officer of the Law.

(Hits intercom.) Hey, Peters: come back. I've changed my mind.

> *(He smiles.* **POLICEWOMAN** *enters.)*

(To **YOUNG SOL.***)* You meet a fine class of people in lock-up.)

> *(***POLICEWOMAN** *takes* **YOUNG SOL** *out.* **SLEZAK** *dials phone.)*

(Into phone.) Creech? Move her. Now. And she'd better not come to the surface…

> *(Lights down on* **SLEZAK**, *rise on defense attorney* **BARRY BARKER** *addressing the press.)*

BARKER. – And this just continues the pattern of police harassment that has characterized this case from the beginning. Who is safe from these people? Are we living in a police state? What's next?

> *(The lighting changes to indicate the press conference is over.)*

> *(***YOUNG SOL** *and* **CALVIN** *confer with the attorney.)*

(To **YOUNG SOL.***)* That was a very nice move.

YOUNG SOL. Right.

BARKER. No, I mean it. Now they've victimized someone besides Calvin.

CALVIN. A white person, you mean.

BARKER. Exactly. *(Sees someone, calls.)* Hey Bill! Bill Kunstler! *(Exits.)*

CALVIN. So you finally got a taste of it, huh? How you like prison, brother?

YOUNG SOL. How do you think? It's not like there was a gang of Jewish guys watching my back. Some Rhodes Scholar named Hector kept threatening to take a closer look at my gold fillings.

CALVIN. *(In a fighter's crouch.)* You tell him where he could go?

YOUNG SOL. No, I told him you were my friend. That made me a big man with the brothers. It almost made Hector dive into the john.

CALVIN. *(Laughs, claps.)* Now you know what it's like to be a New Jersey nigger.

YOUNG SOL. You don't seem to be doing so badly.

CALVIN. Yeah, everyone wants a piece a Mr. Calvin. Invitin' me to fancy parties. Talkin' 'bout namin' a street after me. One minute Maxie's talkin' 'bout runnin' me for Congress, an' the next he's lined up a Hollywood movie, with Muhammad Ali playin' me. Man!

YOUNG SOL. Sure beats being back in a cell, doesn't it? Seriously, Cal, that's all I could think of last night.

CALVIN. You're right about that.

YOUNG SOL. Well, people keep telling me they saw your car fleeing the Cockatoo.

CALVIN. Who are these "people"?

YOUNG SOL. Guys who were there. They swear they saw your car speeding away from the scene.

CALVIN. They may have seen me *driving* away at a fast rate of speed. That doesn't mean I was "fleeing."

> *(Lights fade on* YOUNG SOL *and* CAL *while rising on* ADELE.*)*

ADELE. *(At podium.)* Now I'm not gonna stand here and preach to you 'bout how Afro-American people can't get a fair shake, how they deal us from the bottom o' the deck, then find some way to change the rules whenever we manage to win...

Savage James is no saint. He spent hard time in prison, as a boxer he was often brutal. But as he recounts in his bestselling book, "The Savage Fight" – copies of which are available throughout the hall – "If you come at me in anger, then you'll get anger back. But if you approach me in friendship, then I will be your friend."

If Dr. King were alive today, don't you think he'd be demanding Justice for Calvin James? *(Chants.)* Justice for Calvin! Justice for Calvin! Justice for Calvin!

CROWD. *(Could be voice-over, could be live or a combo.)* Justice for Calvin! Justice for Calvin! Justice for Calvin!

> *(A home phone rings in late 1979. Spot up on* YOUNG SOL, *who picks up.)*

YOUNG SOL. *(Into phone.)* Adele? Is that you, honey? I miss you.

> *(Lights fade on* ADELE, *rise on long-haired blonde woman at pay phone, glancing around.)*

BELINDA. Mr. Eisner?

YOUNG SOL. Yes? Who is this?

BELINDA. Karen Rubins.

YOUNG SOL. Who?

BELINDA. Belinda Clark. *(She looks around warily.)*

YOUNG SOL. Where are you?

BELINDA. At a gas station.

YOUNG SOL. No, I mean –

BELINDA. I know what you mean. You can't tell anyone. Not the press or your own people. It can only be you.

YOUNG SOL. Okay. I understand.

(They both hang up. Lights down on phones, rise on SOL in early 2020 at the webcam.)

SOL. When I was a kid, Danny, the only way to reach anybody was to dial their number on the rotary phone, and then hold on for twenty rings, praying that they would put down their book or emerge from their warm bath in time to answer your call. We didn't even have answering machines! Pathetic, right? And yet we got through! We talked! Now there are so many ways to reach out and touch each other, the only thing missing is a chip in our brains – but still I don't hear from you! Still I don't get a reply! Ella tells me that there's trouble between you and this hood, Terrence. She's afraid for you, Danny! Me too! I want to help, but what can I do if you don't let me? I've actually gone to your club a few times. "Mad Money." Well, okay, I haven't gone inside, but that's only because I have this thing about bouncers and velvet ropes. But I've stood outside, Danny, like some teenybopper craving an autograph. And that big guy you have out there told me that he gave you my message. And still you haven't come out. There's only so long I can wait, even for you. Don't lock me out, Danny, please. Talk to me. Let me inside.

(Spot down on SOL, lights rise on gas station restroom, early 1980: BELINDA and YOUNG SOL in a tight space.)

BELINDA. I want to leave, believe me I do.

YOUNG SOL. Isn't that why you phoned me?

BELINDA. I don't know. I don't know anymore.

YOUNG SOL. Slezak doesn't have jurisdiction here. This is New York.

BELINDA. New York, New Jersey – what's the difference? A cop is a cop. I should know, I married one.

YOUNG SOL. You testified once before...

BELINDA. Yeah, and look what it got me: people spittin' at me in the streets, spray-paintin' "whore" on my parents' garage... I loved my parents, Sol, and I ruined their lives.

YOUNG SOL. You loved Calvin too. You know that he's innocent, right? *(Pause.)*

BELINDA. The first time he came over that night, I wouldn't make love with him. I told him: either me or your wife. Then he phoned me an hour later, and I couldn't resist. If only I had – I wouldn't be a part of this mess.

YOUNG SOL. You're his *alibi*, Belinda. Without you, they may convict him again.

BELINDA. He never even called me. He wrote me a note, like you do when somebody's croaked. I went through hell for that man.

YOUNG SOL. He was in *jail*, Belinda. We're talking life and death here.

BELINDA. What about my life? I'd like to have a life too.

(Looks at her watch.)

Oh shit! I have to go!

YOUNG SOL. What's the rush?

BELINDA. It's 12:15. Creech always checks on me after the Tonight Show.

YOUNG SOL. Creech?

BELINDA. That's my husband.

YOUNG SOL. Unusual name.

BELINDA. Yeah, you should meet him sometime. He's a prince of a guy. A real prince. *(Stands.)* Look, from what I can see, Calvin is doing okay. But if you absolutely can't get by without me...

YOUNG SOL. We can't. I mean, really – we need you.

(*There is a sudden knock at the door.*)

BELINDA. Shit. Oh shit. He's gonna kill me.

YOUNG SOL. Why the hell don't you leave him?

(*There's another knock, louder this time.*)

BELINDA. Jesus. I musta been crazy.

YOUNG SOL. Look, I got you into this... I won't let him hurt you.

BELINDA. Oh really? You think you can stop him?

YOUNG SOL. Just let me handle this.

(**YOUNG SOL** *opens the door: A woman* **MOTORIST** *in a hoodie is there.*)

MOTORIST. Hey, what the fuck? Why don't you do your stuff in the woods? People have to go to the bathroom!

(*Lights down on bathroom, spot rises on* **CALVIN** *in a hotel room.*)

CALVIN. *(On the phone.)* I tell you, Sol, all the craziness I saw in the joint ain't got nothin' on Hollywood! Oh, but ma movie – man, ma movie's gonna be the Black people's movie of all time. I'm gonna reach a hand out to the ghetto, to the babies who be slapped in prison before they can breathe. We be tellin' the truth here, 400 years in the makin'! Even boys like Tyrone, when they see ma movie, they'll stand and feel proud.

> *(Spot fades on **CAL**, lights rise on high-toned hotel lounge: tinkling piano, etc. The red-vested **BARTENDER** polishes the bar.)*

> *(**YOUNG SOL** is counting his change.)*

BARTENDER. Can I get you anything else, sir? Another beer?

YOUNG SOL. Hmm...

> *(Starts to order, then stops himself.)*

No, I don't think so.

> *(**YOUNG SOL** puts a few bills on the bar, starts to leave.*

> *(**ADELE** enters: stunningly dressed, wears makeup, her hair coiffed; kisses **YOUNG SOL**, careful not to smudge her lipstick.)*

ADELE. Sorry, baby. I got here as soon as I could.

YOUNG SOL. Only forty-five minutes late.

ADELE. Is it that late already! My lord.

*(To **BARTENDER**.)* Vodka on the rocks. No, make it a double.

> *(**BARTENDER** pours drink.)*

YOUNG SOL. You could've called.

ADELE. I couldn't! I had a conference call with Mayor Gibson and Jesse Jackson, and a phone conversation with Melvin "Bad-ass" Van Peebles himself. It's ninety-nine percent sure that he's gonna direct Calvin's movie.

YOUNG SOL. Stop talking to me like one of your press people.

ADELE. Well, you do work for Maxie Lazlo now, don't you?

YOUNG SOL. What's that supposed to mean? Adele, we've hardly spoken in weeks. It's been almost a month since we made love –

ADELE. Shhh. Now hold on a minute, baby. This isn't the time or the place.

YOUNG SOL. Then what is? Just tell me. It's ripping me up inside, Adele. I need to know –

>   (**ADELE** *gives him a look, stopping him in his tracks.*)

BARTENDER. One vodka double. (*Gives her the drink.*)

Excuse me, miss, but haven't I seen you on TV? You're with that fighter.

>   (**ADELE** *smiles, sips.*)

YOUNG SOL. Why do I feel all the time like you're dodging me, Adele?

ADELE. I thought we were going to talk strategy, Sol. For the upcoming trial. Okay?

>   (*She puts her hand on his shoulder in a friendly way. This is too much for him, he grabs her, kisses her full on the mouth.*)

Sol!

YOUNG SOL. You know what? This is a hotel. They have rooms. We could rent one.

ADELE. (*Shakes her head.*) Sol...

YOUNG SOL. Don't you miss it as much as I do, Adele?

ADELE. (*Softly.*) Baby... Calvin and I...

YOUNG SOL. *(Going rigid.)* What.

ADELE. You know "what." You're hurt, Sol... I understand. But Cal really needs me.

YOUNG SOL. And I don't? Adele...

ADELE. Don't start with me, baby. It's over.

YOUNG SOL. Is it? How come I didn't know? How come you couldn't tell me?

ADELE. I'm telling you now. *(Pause.)* Believe me, Sol, this is best for all of us.

YOUNG SOL. Really? Wow. That sounds a little self-serving. *(Pause.)* And you think this is a good thing, so close to the trial?

ADELE. Calvin says that if we just follow what we feel in our hearts, it will lead us to –

YOUNG SOL. Fuck what Calvin says! Fuck it!

> *(**ADELE** stands, open-mouthed, keenly aware of the **BARTENDER***'s gaze.)*

Does he love you as much as I do, Adele? Would he give up everything for you?

> *(**ADELE** turns a parting look on **YOUNG SOL**, summons her dignity, exits. **YOUNG SOL** is about to pursue her. **BARTENDER** puts a hand on his shoulder.)*

BARTENDER. You want some advice, mister? Just let her go. You'll live longer.

> *(Lights down on the high-toned bar. Spot up on **SOL** at the webcam.)*

SOL. I should have gone after her, Danny, I see that now. I mean, she hurt me bad. Really bad. But I should have been stronger, I know it. And I blame myself for what happened after.

(Lights fade on **SOL***'s Brooklyn apartment.)*

SAN FRAN DJ. *(Voice-over.)* Well, here's a shocker. Charges were filed this morning in Los Angeles County by Adele Sparks, the plucky spokeswoman for Savage James...

> *(Lights rise on press conference, March 1980:* **ADELE** *addresses the media. Her left arm is in a sling; she seems wobbly, off-kilter.)*

ADELE. Thank you all for coming here today. I devoted over a year of my life to Calvin James, and I'd hoped to stand up here on the day of his vindication... I still believe Cal is not guilty of murder, but I also think he has a problem, a serious problem...

> *(Lights also up on a rival press conference stage left; the lights switch back and forth.)*

BARKER. *(Sits alone.)* In general, we think so little of Ms. Sparks' charges that I have advised my client not even to dignify them with his presence.

ADELE. He attacked me without provocation, practically twisting my left arm out of its socket, displaying a cruelty I had not seen before –

BARKER. I have here a signed affidavit from the Los Angeles physician who examined Ms. Sparks on the morning of March third. He found no evidence of serious injury –

ADELE. I thought long and hard before coming forward, but I believe that in his present state, Calvin James *does* pose a danger. If he doesn't get serious psychiatric help soon, I'm afraid to think what might happen.

BARKER. I also have a copy of a psychiatric outpatient file for Ms. Adele Sparks.

> *(He tosses this hefty file on the table in front of him.)*

ADELE. Please Calvin – I want you to break your cycle of violence. Won't you please get some help?

> *(Pause. Lights down on press briefings, rise on corporate boardroom.)*

> *(**YOUNG SOL** sits, drinking scotch. A bottle is on the table. **MAXIE LAZLO** enters.)*

MAXIE. Did you see the papers today? My God, they killed us. *Killed* us. It couldn't be worse.

YOUNG SOL. No.

MAXIE. And for what? There's absolutely *nothing* backing her up. Not a shred...

YOUNG SOL. I don't know, Maxie.

MAXIE. What d'ya mean, you don't know?

YOUNG SOL. I just don't know anymore...

> *(**CALVIN** stands in the doorway, unseen.)*

MAXIE. *(Swigs booze.)* Okay, this is how we're going to play it: the bitch was trying to get money. Right. He wanted to get rid of her, but she wouldn't go without cash. When he wouldn't pay it –

YOUNG SOL. No can do, Maxie.

MAXIE. What?

YOUNG SOL. That dog won't hunt. That bird won't fly. That moose won't...

MAXIE. Come on.

YOUNG SOL. You should never have made her files public.

MAXIE. What's wrong with you? You want them to win?

> *(**CALVIN** applauds from the doorway.)*

Hey Cal! Buddy! Didja hear that? I'm tryin' to keep your ass outta the fire, while this little Yeshiva boy –

CALVIN. He's right.

MAXIE. What?

CALVIN. No more smoke an' mirrors, Maxie.

MAXIE. Maybe you're not really grasping the situation. You just threw Slezak a forward pass. He's not gonna let the ball drop.

CALVIN. Then I gotta deal with that, don't I?

MAXIE. Yeah, that's really good. What are the two a you gonna do? Write a really *harsh* letter?

CALVIN. We'll think of something...that is, if Sol still believes.

MAXIE. Oh yeah. Mr. Calvin Savage Number One Contender for life without parole! *(Grabs his coat.)* That'll teach me to take on a freebie.

(He exits. **CAL** *approaches* **YOUNG SOL.***)*

CALVIN. So what's the story, brother? You give up on Cal too?

YOUNG SOL. Yup.

CALVIN. Well, that's honest anyway. *(Pause.)* Looks like my committee done slimmed down a little.

YOUNG SOL. Yeah. You sure know how to empty a room.

CALVIN. I do at that, don't I? Hey, pass me that bottle.

YOUNG SOL. No.

CALVIN. You gave it to Maxie.

YOUNG SOL. How could you *do* something like that, Cal? How could you...

CALVIN. Ya know, I wish just for once you was sittin' here, and I was lookin' like that down at you... Wish it was me tryin' to save yo' ass.

YOUNG SOL. Yeah, that would be a switch.

CALVIN. Wish I could ride to *yo'* rescue, the shining Black knight.

YOUNG SOL. Funny how it's always *your* ass that's in the sling, always *you* who's been set up, while everyone else is against you...

CALVIN. Not you, brother. Not you an' Tyrone.

YOUNG SOL. Oh, don't give me that. Tyrone's a petty thief and a pathological liar.

CALVIN. That *was* Tyrone, before I had a chance to –

YOUNG SOL. Tyrone said – He called me up and told me –

CALVIN. What?

(Pause. Then **YOUNG SOL** *pivots away from this.)*

YOUNG SOL. And what about Adele? Wasn't she on your side too? The last I saw, she was playing Betty Shabazz to your Malcolm X.

CALVIN. That's cruel, bro. But I guess I deserve it. An' I done you wrong too. Sorry, man. I shoulda left that woman alone. *(Puts out his hand.)*

YOUNG SOL. Just get away from me. You were just a mistake.

CALVIN. Can't blame ya, I guess... You weren't wrong though. Not about that Jewish couple. Always thought that was brave o' you. Ya know – seein' as how you're Jewish.

YOUNG SOL. Adele *worshipped* you, Cal. She wouldn't turn on you without cause.

CALVIN. What can I say, bro? Sometimes worship is the worst form a love.

YOUNG SOL. That's no reason to beat her.

CALVIN. I fucked up, man. Okay? I fucked up. But I didn't beat her.

YOUNG SOL. Oh no?

CALVIN. Hey, I was just holding on to keep her away. To keep her from scratching my eyes out. All because I said that I didn't need a spokeswoman anymore, I could speak for myself.

YOUNG SOL. *(Slurs his words.)* I want to hear she say.

CALVIN. What? Man, you can't even drink right.

YOUNG SOL. *(Passes the bottle.)* Okay. Show me.

> (**CALVIN** *takes a big swig.*)

CALVIN. That's how it went down, man. Ask her yourself. What else can I tell you?

> (**CALVIN** *takes another swig, slams the bottle back down on the table.*)

I got a feeling about you, man. Always have. You're the one guy I can count on.

YOUNG SOL. Oh yeah? What makes you think that?

CALVIN. You are the one guy who can figure this out.

> *(Points to his heart.)*

I feel that in here. And this has never steered me wrong. Never.

> *(Lights fade on the boardroom, rise on* **SOL** *addressing his webcam.)*

SOL. And he was right, Danny. I figured it out. That's right, I did. You want to know how your dad went all Sherlock Holmes on this case when everyone else was baffled? No, you probably don't. And the truth is, it wasn't really all that exciting. I just went back and looked over all the evidence, and it was obvious. Obvious! There was a guy that night in the Cockatoo – the bar that the old couple went into – who had been left out of the police report. Not the first draft, but the second draft. The one they gave the press. And so once I got a copy of that first draft from Danny Rooks... Well...

(Lights rise on cellblock room, May 1980: **TYRONE** *at table,* **YOUNG SOL** *facing him,* **GUARD 2** *in back.)*

YOUNG SOL. So, Tyrone: I hear you have a parole hearing coming up?

TYRONE. Yup. Keepin' my fingers crossed.

YOUNG SOL. You could be out in what – five, six weeks? You'll miss the trial.

TYRONE. Ain't that a shame? After all the work I done for Cal?

YOUNG SOL. Then again, the last time we spoke, you told me that Calvin was guilty.

TYRONE. Aw, I was just messin' with you, brother Sol. You didn't take me serious, did you?

YOUNG SOL. I take you very seriously, brother Tyrone.

TYRONE. Ha. Good to know. Anythin' in partic'lar you wanted ta ask me? I'm feelin' a bit unda th' weather today.

YOUNG SOL. So sorry to hear that.

TYRONE. Ain't been gettin' ma beauty sleep lately.

YOUNG SOL. Got a lot on your mind?

TYRONE. Well, you know, this hearin'...an' I'm fearful for Calvin.

YOUNG SOL. You should be. Even with Belinda Clark testifying, it doesn't look great.

TYRONE. Ain't that a shame?

YOUNG SOL. Yes. It certainly is...

> (YOUNG SOL *brings over an extra chair.*
> CALVIN *enters.*)

CALVIN. *(Stands over* TYRONE.*)* Hey Tyrone.

TYRONE. Calvin! Thought you forgot all 'bout ol' Tyrone!

CALVIN. I ain't forgot you. Heard you're gettin' out early.

TYRONE. Ain't certain yet... How come you don't sit down,
Calvin? We just brothers here.

CALVIN. How come you do me like that, youngblood?

TYRONE. Whatchu talkin' 'bout? What these people been
tellin' ya? You got no better frien' than Tyrone! *(Pause.)*
Hey guard! I wanna go!

YOUNG SOL. We know, Tyrone.

TYRONE. You know what?

YOUNG SOL. We know you murdered that couple.

TYRONE. Bullshit! Cal –

CALVIN. How come you do me like that, brother?

TYRONE. Why you listen to this ugly white boy? That cuts
me, Cal. That really cuts... Hey guard! Get off yo' fat
ass!

> (GUARD 2 *approaches.*)

CALVIN. You best keep lookin' over your shoulder,
youngblood, 'cause Savage James will be there...

TYRONE. You washed-up nigger. I twisted you every which
way. You been Tyrone's bitch.

> *(He grins at* CALVIN. CALVIN *feints with his
> right,* TYRONE *flinches.*)

CALVIN. *(To* YOUNG SOL.*)* Didja get that?

(**YOUNG SOL** *takes out his tape recorder, nods.*)

TYRONE. You think you so hot... I'm laughin' at you. You hear me? I'm laughin'! Laughin'!

> *(Lights down on prison, rise on* **SLEZAK** *at Police HQ. Intercom buzzes.)*

SLEZAK. *(Into intercom.)* Yeah?

POLICEWOMAN. *(Voice-over.)* That guy's here again. Eisner.

SLEZAK. Tell 'im I'm busy.

POLICEWOMAN. *(Voice-over.)* He says it's important, sir.

SLEZAK. On second thought bring him in. You come too.

> *(***SLEZAK** *takes out a piece of paper, puts it in reach.)*

> *(***POLICEWOMAN** *enters with* **YOUNG SOL.***)*

Okay: now frisk him for a recorder.

YOUNG SOL. I'm allowed to have one.

SLEZAK. Not if I say you're not.

> *(***YOUNG SOL** *gives his machine to* **POLICEWOMAN.***)*

Go on. Keep searching.

YOUNG SOL. This is a violation of my civil rights.

SLEZAK. Take it up with your congressman.

> *(***POLICEWOMAN** *indicates that* **SOL** *is clean.)*

Okay, you can go.

> *(***POLICEWOMAN** *turns to exit.)*

SOL. Don't you wanta strip-search me?

SLEZAK. Tempting, huh? Maybe some other time.

(POLICEWOMAN exits.)

YOUNG SOL. *(Sits.)* Feeling pretty good about things, huh?

SLEZAK. Oh yeah.

YOUNG SOL. Why is this so *personal*, huh? What did Cal do to you?

SLEZAK. You gotta lot of balls comin' in here a week before the trial and askin' something like that... I guess that's why I like you.

YOUNG SOL. If you like me so much, why won't you answer my questions?

SLEZAK. Oh, and that little stunt you and your "bro" pulled on Tyrone at Trenton State. Now that was nifty. Too bad you came up empty.

YOUNG SOL. We'll see.

SLEZAK. You know I have something here with your name on it...a sworn deposition from a guard at County lock-up. Says you paid Lugo twenty bucks for his recantation. That's bribery, friend.

YOUNG SOL. You can't make that stick.

SLEZAK. I could if I wanted to, and we both know it. But I don't want to.

(SLEZAK tears up the deposition.)

I wanta see the look on your face when Savage goes down again.

YOUNG SOL. What's wrong with you, Slezak? Doesn't it mean anything to you to get the right man?

SLEZAK. Oh I got the right man. I mean, what is Tyrone Bell to me, more or less? But Savage James – now there's a man who can bring all the Tyrones *together*. See what I mean? Hey, my job is to protect the taxpayers from danger. And I will do it – like your friend Malcolm X said – "By Any Means Necessary"...

YOUNG SOL. Okay. But what I don't understand is how a lowly detective like you could pull this off. Just between us, was the upper brass in on this too?

SLEZAK. Just between us, yeah...that's funny. People see what they want to see, Sol. Nobody wants to see Savage James walk. Nobody who matters, that is.

(**SLEZAK** *hits the intercom button. Lights down on Police HQ.*)

(**YOUNG SOL** *stands, walks away. Lights rise on* **CREECH**, *who approaches.*)

CREECH. *(A rogue cop.)* Hey. You Solomon Eisner?

YOUNG SOL. Who wants to know?

CREECH. My friends call me Creech.

YOUNG SOL. Really? Then I'll call you something else.

CREECH. You do that. You're smaller than I thought.

YOUNG SOL. And you're exactly as I pictured you. Just shows to go you, I guess.

Belinda tells me you're quite a husband.

CREECH. That's right. I love my wife.

YOUNG SOL. Oh yeah?

CREECH. You tell her that, okay? I love her. I truly do. Oh – and tell her not to testify.

YOUNG SOL. Or what?

(**CREECH** *smiles, shakes his head. Lights fade on* **CREECH**.)

(*Lights rise on a gloomy hotel room:* **ADELE** *sits in a rickety chair, dressed in a drab housecoat, looking out the window.* **YOUNG SOL** *enters.*)

YOUNG SOL. Adele? Adele?

ADELE. How'd you find me?

YOUNG SOL. You know me: I'm persistent.

ADELE. That's true.

YOUNG SOL. I had to wait 'til that guard took a break... Come on, Adele. Let's get out of here.

ADELE. You know I can't do that.

YOUNG SOL. Why not?

ADELE. Does he know where I am too?

YOUNG SOL. I haven't told him.

ADELE. Good. You're not lying now?

YOUNG SOL. Why can't the two of you patch this thing up? For old times' sake.

ADELE. Too late for that. I've gone on TV, I've been interviewed in the papers.

YOUNG SOL. Just say it was a lovers' quarrel, that's all.

ADELE. Jesse Jackson said nice things about me. Muhammad Ali asked me out. How's it gonna look if I go back on this now?

YOUNG SOL. Like you're a person who cares more about Justice than what people think. Please come with me, Adele. It kills me to see you like this. Please let me help you.

> (**YOUNG SOL** *reaches out.* **ADELE** *leans forward, takes his hand.*)

ADELE. You've been on my mind, Sol. I've got something to tell you.

YOUNG SOL. Look, we can apologize to each other later. For right now –

ADELE. I'm pregnant.

YOUNG SOL. What?

ADELE. It's yours. Counting back to the time...to the start... it's your baby.

YOUNG SOL. Adele...

ADELE. I was going through so much for a while, and I just couldn't think straight...and now it's too far along. I'm sure it's the last thing you want.

YOUNG SOL. No. I – I –

ADELE. I just messed everything up, baby, I messed up so bad... *(She cries.)*

I'm sorry, baby, so sorry... What can I do now?

YOUNG SOL. Adele, honey, don't do this. We'll find a way.

> *(***ROOKS,** **SOL***'s cop on the inside, emerges from the shadows.)*

ROOKS. Sol. I think I hear someone coming.

> *(***YOUNG SOL** *waves him away.)*

ADELE. What's that?

YOUNG SOL. Nothing. Just a friend. He's on lookout.

ROOKS. We gotta get out of here now!

ADELE. Why you bring your white friends here with you? You afraid of Adele? You think I'm gonna *hurt* you?

YOUNG SOL. Come on, Adele. Come with me.

ADELE. Better get outta here, white boy, before I start screamin'!

YOUNG SOL. I love you, Adele...

> *(***ADELE** *screams.)*

(**ROOKS** *pulls* **YOUNG SOL** *away, they exit.*)

(*Lights down on the gloomy hotel room.*)

(*The sound of a lock turning, being opened by a key.*)

(*Lights rise on the door unit, February 2020.* **SOL** *has just opened his front door to find* **DANNY** *sitting on the sofa, dressed in a less flashy fashion than before.*)

DANNY. Tell me about Moms.

SOL. Why?

DANNY. Why not? She was my moms, wasn't she? She was in my dream last night.

She didn't look so good. She couldn't stop crying.

SOL. What was she crying about? How do you know it was her?

DANNY. She's my moms.

SOL. Well... She was beautiful. Forceful. Very smart. Sexy.

DANNY. Oh, so she was a saint?

SOL. Did you hear me say "sexy"?

DANNY. Why did she kill herself?

SOL. Danny.

DANNY. You never told me anything, man. I need to know.

SOL. She had problems, okay? Depression. It's a disease.

DANNY. Hey, I taught high school. In New York City. I know about depression. But that doesn't make it okay to off yourself and have your ten-year-old son walk into the kitchen and see his mom's blood spattered all over the wall because you were really really sad. That's not a memory that any kid should have to carry around with him.

SOL. You're right, but she was a broken person by then. And you kept her alive for those years. You did. Without you –

DANNY. But it wasn't without me. It wasn't. And I can't forgive that.

SOL. She loved you beyond everything. You were the best part of her.

DANNY. Bullshit, old man. When I ask you for the truth, then give it to me straight. Don't hand me some fucking Hallmark card...

SOL. It is the truth, Danny. She loved you, but she couldn't take care of you.

She couldn't take care of herself.

DANNY. What about the two of you?

SOL. What about us?

DANNY. I remember you a little bit when I was like five, and then hardly at all until after she died.

SOL. It's true, I took care of you for six months when she... had a bad stretch. I always wondered if you'd remember that.

DANNY. There you go again, old man. "Had a bad stretch"... what the fuck is that?

(**SOL** *shrugs*.)

It was crack, wasn't it? She was using.

(**SOL** *nods*.)

Why didn't you stop her?

SOL. I tried, Danny. You have to believe me. I tried. But she wouldn't let me get close enough.

DANNY. I don't have to believe anything. And maybe you should have tried harder, old man.

SOL. I loved her, Danny, I did, but every time I managed to get close to her again, then she'd really go off the deep end. I didn't know what to do.

DANNY. Then fuck the bitch!

SOL. Danny!

DANNY. Fuck her! Anyone who could blow her brains out like that, practically in front of her only child... I'm glad that she's dead.

SOL. Come on, Danny, you're better than that.

DANNY. Who says? You don't know me. You don't know a goddamn thing about me.

SOL. Oh please. There's not a lot that I know in this world, but I know you.

DANNY. Maybe you think you do.

SOL. Anyway, I won't have you disrespecting your mother. She went through a lot.

DANNY. Oh please. Disrespect? Don't cry for me, bitch! You were weak! Your tears make me sick!

SOL. Danny! There's so much more to it. That's why I've been making these tapes.

DANNY. Fuck you, old man. Fuck your tapes! Who needs them? Who needs the past?

SOL. Danny.

DANNY. That shit has happened already. It's over. I'm all about *now*!

SOL. You don't mean that.

DANNY. This is *my* time! I'm *happening*! And I don't need anyone else!

(*SOL tries to put his arms around* **DANNY**, *but* **DANNY** *breaks away, exits.* **SOL** *is devastated, holds his head in his hands. Then looks up.*)

SOL. *(To webcam.)* The past does matter, Danny. It has to. It's all I have. It's all any of us really ends up with.

> *(Lights fade on Sol's apartment. In the darkness:)*

RADIO NEWS. *(Voice-over.)* Though once a spokeswoman for Mr. James, Adele Sparks is now listed as a witness for the prosecution –

TV REPORTER 3. Judge Gordon ruled today that a tape recording of Tyrone Bell made by the defense has no legal bearing.

RADIO NEWS. *(Voice-over.)* Sources in the prosecutor's offices have hinted that Ms. Sparks would only be called as a rebuttal witness, should Mr. James testify –

> *(We hear the offstage sound of a judge's gavel.)*

> *(**BARKER** enters, arguing with **CALVIN** and **YOUNG SOL**.)*

BARKER. And I tell you, it would be suicide!

CALVIN. Then what have I come all this way for?

YOUNG SOL. Exactly.

CALVIN. How could I live with myself?

BARKER. Do you want my legal opinion, or don't you?

YOUNG SOL. That's not the issue. Cal is on trial here –

BARKER. And I am trying to win this case. I think we have a good chance.

YOUNG SOL. They have to see him fight for himself. That jury –

BARKER. Hey, this isn't "Rocky," alright? I like movies too, but you saw what they did to Belinda Clark.

CALVIN. She stood up to them!

YOUNG SOL. That's right!

BARKER. They made her look like the goddamn Whore of
Babylon.

CALVIN. So? She toughed it out. Now it's my turn.

BARKER. I couldn't protect you up there, Calvin. And who
knows what Adele's going to testify to? Once she gets
up there and starts talking about the Committee, and
you twisting her arm –

CALVIN. I don't want your protection! I'll fight my own
fight.

> *(Pause: lights rise also on* **SLEZAK** *and* **ADELE**,
> *stage right.)*

SLEZAK. You're gonna do it.

ADELE. I can't.

SLEZAK. Oh, I think you can.

> *(***ADELE*** *shakes her head.)*

Just think about it.

ADELE. Everything's gotten so twisted around... I don't
know what I believe anymore...

SLEZAK. Oh, I think you do.

> *(The focus shifts back to* **YOUNG SOL** *and*
> **CALVIN** *and* **BARKER**.)*

YOUNG SOL. It's all come down to this, Cal. You asked me
to believe in you. Well I have. And I do.

> *(***YOUNG SOL** *and* **CAL** *exchange a handshake.)*

BARKER. It's a bad idea! There are too many things that
could damage our case!

CALVIN. No. It's down to me. I'm the only one that's got
the truth, an' it has to be spoken.

*(The focus shifts again to **SLEZAK** and **ADELE**.)*

ADELE. You don't really need me, do you? You have a strong case...

SLEZAK. Are you gonna let him get the last word again? Are you gonna let Savage speak while you're kept silent? Are you gonna let him make you look like a joke again?

> *(**CALVIN** steps downstage and takes a long look at **ADELE**. She turns, looks directly at him.)*

ADELE. I will not do it.

> *(Lights down on the two groups, rise on **CAL**.)*

CALVIN. *(Walks to witness chair, sits down, faces front.)* I am not a perfect man, or even a good one. I have done many bad things in my lifetime, made many mistakes, done injury to many who didn't deserve it, including my own family, which hurts most of all. I have used the gift of strength that God gave me to inflict pain on others – of this I stand guilty before this court, and the higher court too. And maybe that's how these things work, maybe I was being punished for all them other things. But as to the crime of which I'm accused here – I am *not* guilty. This State has blood on its hands.

WOMAN TV REPORTER. *(Speaks into her microphone.)* Hello, this is Wendy Bird reporting from the Savage James trial, where there has been a major turnaround, sparked by Mr. James's own testimony three days ago. His former spokeswoman, Adele Sparks, has now come forward to say that she was instructed to lie on the witness stand by Detective Frank Slezak of the Newark Police.

> *(Lights rise on **SLEZAK** downstage right, on his desk phone.)*

SLEZAK. *(Into phone.)* Look, Creech, this is what we do right now – nothing. You got that? Zip. Zero. Nada. Just take it easy, okay? They may still convict him, who knows? Don't do anything stupid. You hear me? Creech? Creech?

> *(Lights fade on **SLEZAK**, rise again outside the courthouse.)*

CROWD. *(Voice-over: a general buzz of excitement plus random shouts.)* "We love you, Savage!" "The trial was rigged!" "We want justice!" "Justice for Savage!"

WOMAN TV REPORTER. I think it's fair to say that the pendulum of public opinion has once again swung solidly into Mr. James's corner.

CROWD. *(Voice-over, chants.)* Savage! Savage! Savage! Savage!

WOMAN TV REPORTER. Do you hear that? These people just can't get enough of him! He should be coming back from the recess any minute... Wait. I think I can see him.

> *(Spot rises on **CREECH**, who approaches **CALVIN** like a fan, his hand out.)*

CREECH. Hey Savage.

CALVIN. Hey Buddy, how's it goin'?

CREECH. This is for Belinda.

> *(**CREECH** takes a gun from his jacket pocket, shoots twice at **CAL**.)*
>
> *(Sounds of screams and chaos ensuing in the crowd.)*

WOMAN TV REPORTER. Oh my God! He's been hit. Savage is bleeding. Somebody help him! Somebody!

(A cell phone rings in Sol's apartment, February 2020. Lights down on **REPORTER**, *rise on* **SOL** *at his webcam and* **ELLA** *on the street.)*

SOL. *(Answers cell phone.)* Hello?

ELLA. *(On cell phone.)* Sol! Oh thank God! It's Ella. I tried to reach you. Over and over.

SOL. *(On phone.)* I was making my tapes. I had the phone turned off.

ELLA. *(On phone.)* You shouldn't do that, Sol. People are trying to call you.

SOL. *(Refers to the tape.)* It was so hard for me to tell about his death.

ELLA. *(Into phone.)* What? Whose death? You got a call from the hospital?

SOL. *(Into phone.)* No. What's the matter?

ELLA. *(Into phone.)* It's Danny.

(Pause. Lights down on Sol's apartment, rise on the hospital room.)

(**DANNY** *is in a wheelchair, a bandage around his head.* **SOL** *enters.)*

DANNY. You were right, Pops! I am better than that! I didn't think I was, but I am!

SOL. Just take it easy, Danny. Lie back.

DANNY. Terrence came at me with a gun. He shot me, then I took it away.

I had my finger on the trigger to kill him. And then I heard your words in my head.

"You're better than that." And I am.

SOL. I know you are, Danny. I always knew that.

DANNY. I feel so bad about Moms now. It wasn't all her fault. I can see that.

(ADELE *enters, looks at* SOL.)

ADELE. Are you going to tell him now?

SOL. *(To* ADELE.*)* Yes.

ADELE. Are you going to tell him everything?

DANNY. Pops?

SOL. I'm sorry, Danny. So sorry.

DANNY. For what?

SOL. I should have been a better dad. I should have tried harder.

It was just... You reminded me so much of her. I couldn't take it.

ADELE. Poor you.

DANNY. I can see that, Pops. Sure.

ADELE. You're not going to tell him, are you?

DANNY. Just stay in my corner, okay?

SOL. I'm not going anywhere, Danny.

(SOL *puts his arms around* DANNY.)

ADELE. That's right, hold on to him like the coward you are.

SOL. *(To* DANNY.*)* I'll be right here.

DANNY. Thanks, Pops.

ADELE. Your tapes are a joke. We remember what we want to remember, that's all.

SOL. *(To* ADELE.*)* Oh, I remember.

DANNY. You remember what?

SOL. When your mom came back from her last time at rehab, and she was so hopeful, and all she wanted was a kind word from me. Instead I lashed out.

ADELE. You said, "If you can't stay clean this time, then just put yourself out of your misery. Stop dragging Danny and the rest of us down with you."

SOL. I killed her.

DANNY. Pops!

SOL. I might as well have put that gun in her mouth.

DANNY. She pulled the trigger, Pops. She did.

(**SOL** *shakes his head.*)

You just reminded me of something. When I was in surgery, I saw her again. Moms. But she wasn't crying this time. She was smiling. I think she forgives you, Pops. I really do.

SOL. Thank you for that, Danny. Thank you.

*(He hugs **DANNY**.)*

DANNY. I think we're gonna be okay this time, Pops.

SOL. Yes?

DANNY. I think you and I have a chance to start over.

SOL. I hope so, Danny. I hope so.

(Lights fade slowly to black.)

End of Play